H‍o... o,

M... u?

For Jill and Ray

Billy   die Frost

ROAR

A beautiful envelope arrived.

Gnu ripped it open with his teeth.

It was an invitation to tea
WITH THE QUEEN!

Gnu was going to have to learn some manners!

"How do you do?"

"How do you do?"

"And how do you do to you too?"

"Woof," woofed the dog.

"As fine manners as I ever did see," exclaimed Gnu.

"I shall add them to my repertoire!"

"Woof," woofed Gnu. "Woof, woof, WOOF!"
and he sat up on his hind legs and begged.

"Caw," cawed the raven.
"What exquisite manners!"
said Gnu. "Let me try!"

"Caw," cawed Gnu.

"Caw, caw, CAW!" and his spindly legs flapped like wings with all their might.

"Glug,"
glugged the fish.

"Such eloquence," raved Gnu.
"I should like to try!"

"Glug,"

glugged Gnu as he flopped about in the river.

"Glug,
glug,
GLUG!"

"ROAR!"
roared the dinosaur.

"Oh my!" said Gnu.
"I simply must try that!"

"Roar," roared Gnu as loud as he possibly could.

"Roar, roar, ROAR!"

"How refined!" praised Gnu. "May I try?"

"Neigh," neighed Gnu.
He shook his mane and
he stamped his hoof.

"Neigh,

neigh,

NEIGH!"

"Pfffffft," raspberried the little girl.

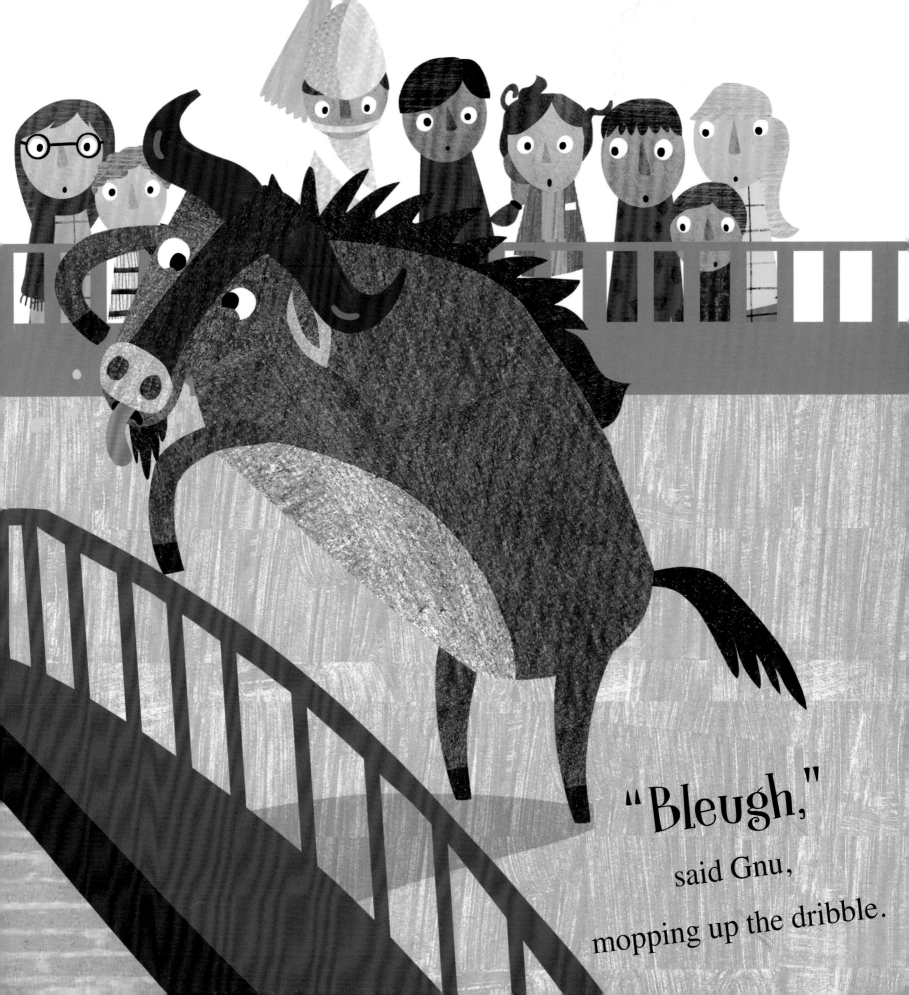

"Bleugh,"
said Gnu,
mopping up the dribble.

"How do you do, Mr Gnu?" said the Queen.
"I hear you are practising your manners."

Mr Gnu bowed as low as he could.

And then he stuck out his tongue. "Pffft!"

"Pffft, Pffft, PFFFT!!!"

The End

How Do You Do, Mr Gnu?
An original concept by author Billy Coughlan
© Billy Coughlan
Illustrated by Maddie Frost

MAVERICK ARTS PUBLISHING LTD
Studio 3A, City Business Centre, 6 Brighton Road, Horsham, West Sussex, RH13 5BB
© Maverick Arts Publishing Limited   +44 (0)1403 256941

Published March 2017

A CIP catalogue record for this book is available at the British Library.

ISBN 978-1-84886-242-5

Maveric
arts publishing
www.maverickbooks.co.uk